GNARLED BONES AND OTHER STORIES

Tam May

Gnarled Bones And Other Stories
Tam May

Published by Dreambook Press.

Click or visit:
www.tammayauthor.com

Cover Design © 2017 by Dreambook Press. Photo Credit: *Portrait Of An Old Woman*, Louise De Hern, 1888, Stedelijk Museum, Belgium: Spinster/ Wikimedia Commons/PD Old 80

ISBN: 978-0-9981979-0-6 (Print)
ISBN: 978-0-9981979-1-3 (ebook)

To Aila and Becky for their confidence in me as a writer and their enthusiastic support of my work.

Mother of Mischief

Her younger brothers used to call her Mother of Mischief. In the smoky town of Rawlins where their father had owned a jewelry repair shop and their mother cooked franks and beans over an iron stove, Marie was left to tend to her brothers after school. They were five and ten years younger than she and she watched over them with a maternal eye, her ankle thrust forward and her hands close to her hips. More times than not, they escaped into the rascality of spirited little boys. They ran across the grain-colored carpet in winter boots caked with mud, shot spitballs at unsteady dishes sitting on the rack, and rolled marbles at the feet of people passing on the street from the safe shield of the fur tree. As they grew older they learned to watch for the beginnings of the pose like the hand reaching towards the hip and the stone ankle. As men, they appreciated Marie's worrisome eye, comparing it to the glassy looks their ex-wives gave them. They still felt that she was pacing the ground as she had when they were boys, watching at the window for their pale blue bicycles to emerge from over the hill. They were grateful that in the midst of their father's failing eyesight, their mother's crooked back, and the silent dinners with their exhausted parents, there had been one person who tried to curtail their mischief with a loving conscience.

At nineteen, Marie married a man who, like her father, was in the jewelry business. They lived modestly in a small apartment house on Rawlins' main street. Walter's shop was a short distance away and in the late afternoon, when the sun sent sparks flying off the jewelry in the front window, Marie peered out, her anxious hand against her hip and her bent knee pressed on the parapet.

At first he thought her concern was sweet and his lethargic mind was content. Then her alert eye began to disturb him. Its perpetual gaze down into the shop window agonized him and he fought with her, demanding to know just what she thought he was doing in the shop in the late afternoon shadow that she should be scrutinizing him. Marie had no answer. All she could say was, "I'm Mother of Mischief and that's what I do."

One afternoon, after she had just placed a hot pie to cool, she looked out the window, wiping her hands on a towel. She saw her husband on his stool, kneeling over a teenage girl who was finishing her final year at Rawlins High School. A few months later, during a dinner of pot roast and poached pears, he announced he had been having an affair with the girl for months and now that she turned eighteen he intended to divorce Marie so he could marry her.

Marie took the advice of her brothers. She left Rawlins and moved to the West Coast, settling in the largest and most oblivious city she could find. Los Angeles stood sprawled glossy streets that spilled into the ocean. The monstrosity of the city took strange hold of her. As she stood above it her first night, the soft wind cutting through the scent of citrus blossoms and the lights a maze of glitter and hope, she let go of her anxious eye, her stiff hip and her protruding ankle. She saw clearly. Men had liquid eyes and liquid morals, trapped in their lies and fallacies. She became angry for the first time in her life. She was not angry at the men like her mother when back pain led her into spiraling bitterness before she died, but angry at herself for willingly becoming the woman responsible for those who transformed life into mischief instead of going out and transforming life herself.

She vowed she would never be Mother of Mischief again.

*

She entered the university in the Women's Studies program. Because of the prudent alimony she received from Walter, she had no choice but to apply to the student organization for a shared apartment.

They sent her to a pretty Spanish building on

a quiet side street. It was only after she accepted, without looking too judiciously at the names of the other inhabitants that she realized her roommates were three young men, one of them younger than her youngest brother.

To be fair, they demanded nothing of her. There were two bathrooms, one small and one large, and they offered to let her have the large one all to herself. They participated in the cooking and the housework and kept the volume of their music down. She found herself warming to the scraggly morning faces and while she allowed none of them to coax out the casting eye and protruding hip, they sometimes sat down to a late breakfast with her on Sunday mornings and talked about their studies, their part-time jobs and their friends.

At the end of her first year, one of the boys left and they applied for a new roommate. They wanted to take in a woman but the applicants were all men. They decided on Henry.

At nineteen, Henry was the youngest in the household and some kind of mechanical genius who had delayed going to college because of the death of his mother. Marie was the last one in the house to meet him. He was already caught in the chaos of unpacking boxes when she walked in. His back was to her as he opened a wooden chest and began pulling out pictures. He lined them up on the desk. She could see he was painfully thin with the emaciation of one whose meals always left him just a little bit hungry. His shoulders and back would have been comfortably muscular with good nourishing. The slim boy touched a nerve in her, reminding her of her youngest brother who couldn't tolerate anything but franks and beans until he was twenty.

He turned around then, a picture held to his chest. He had the beauty of a hastily left youth but there was wisdom in his copper eyes. They were wide, not with innocence but with pain and panic.

She approached the desk. The pictures included a woman, a blond older woman with a pleasant smiling face. The eyes matched Henry's, bold and copper.

"You must have loved her very much," she said in a quiet voice.

She felt Henry's gaze on her as she left the room, closing the door behind her, but not completely. She left a crack open for air, for welcome.

They both ate earlier than the others, so they were often alone for breakfast. He spoke of his mother, of her mopping floors twelve hours a day, coughing from the toxic cleansers. He told Marie of the nickels his mother put in a jar for him at night when he was asleep. Those nickels, he said, were now buying his books and his meals. He spoke of his father who had stayed behind in Russia, of remote family in Siberia, of his desire to be a poet and a painter after he had made all the money he could from mechanical engineering.

Marie listened with the ease of a woman who was used to absorbing troubles. She couldn't shut herself away as she did when the other boys talked about their mothers or their girlfriends. He picked his words carefully as if they were ripe apples off a tree, aware of the sadness they left behind. The other men thought he was too melancholy and called him Gloom Boy. They tried to provoke laughter or anger from him by sandpapering his hair over his forehead like a child or by surrounding him, barking like dogs. He turned into himself, the bone hollow in his cheeks. Marie scolded them for teasing him.

He began going out alone at night in the summer. At first Marie would occupy herself with extra books and summer classes. The other young men went out as well and would come in a little after midnight, smelling faintly of beer and perfume. Henry would stay away, sometimes until dawn. He would come in, lost in the marrow of his boned face like a skeleton as he went down the hall. Sometimes she thought she could hear the gasp of tears but usually he was silent, smelling sharp from the mints that were constantly dissolving under his tongue.

In spite of the vow she made into the black city her first night, the dye had cast her as Mother of Mischief. She would wait until the others settled into bed and drape a shawl worn thin by her mother across her shoulders. She would wander the main road near the school where students went to displace their anxieties in drink and dance. She peered through the doorways of bars and clubs, her sultry eye studying the students who had begun their descent into oblivion.

Eventually she would find him but never in the same place. He was unlike most students who had their haunts. He seemed to wander into any place, a misty shadow alone in a corner. At times, a mug sat on the table, a clean mug. She found out from the bartenders that most nights he paid for an empty glass. The sprawling glitter of revolving lights would reflect against the hollows of his face, turning his skin green, red, and blue. He would be staring at some phantom across the table, his eyes glossy and transfixed. Marie would approach him and hold out her hand. They would walk home slowly, oblivious to the students and the crowds in the streets. Marie led Henry like a mother leading her little boy home after a tragedy.

At other times, she would find him with eyes wide and furious with despair over a bottle of scotch that he consumed down to the bottom. A few women surrounded him, trying to touch the delicate rim of his cheeks and the sweetness of his Russian bone structure. Marie would watch only for a moment, pain making her mouth taste bitter like poison. She would flee home and wait, sitting up in bed with the door closed, listening for his heavy walk up the stairs.

One night the door of her bedroom opened and he came wavering in like a willow in the wind. Without looking at her, he said, "Mother of Mischief, Mother of Panic. Will you ever stop?"

She froze as the door shut with a soft scratch.

Bracelets

Five men entered the circus like overgrown children. Their ages ranged between thirty and thirty-five and their faces still held on to a boyish gaze. One of them, a man six foot three and weighing almost three hundred pounds, shouted, "Is this fun? Is this fun?" His face looked half-melted and his eyes were vague.

Isabelle followed them on the arm of her friend Mickey. She looked like a wild flower among redwoods. Usually, she chose the solid pose of a woman reluctantly subdued. But with Mickey she could be lively, shooting snide remarks and observations about people that pierced the very core of their fears and joys. She was more astute than unkind.

No one knew she and Mickey were friends even though they worked in the same office. Isabelle's sweet voice, petite figure, and misty smile made people believe she needed guidance. All her life people had tried to guide her, just as they did now in her job as a mailroom secretary, touching her shoulder and giving liberal advice on how to work extra hard so that she might be an executive assistant some day. They were determined to teach her how to be indispensable and grow a career among the files and the phone lines. She smiled and nodded at them but when she was alone with Mickey, walking along the beach or in

Golden Gate Park, she spat at them. Mickey had taught her how to spit and she shot great wads of saliva into the mud or wet sand. Mickey roared with a great childish laugh, his dark hair curling against his high cheeks and his dark eyes sparkling like rock candy.

Mickey worked in the mailroom too and people talked down to him because he quit school to read about life on his own. He found a list of the one hundred greatest books in the world when he was fourteen and he had been reading through it ever since.

"Don't you get bored sometimes?" Isabelle asked him.

"How can you be bored inside someone else's imagination?" He answered her.

He always spoke like that, thoughtful and intense. Lately, Isabelle had been encouraging him to write his own poetry but he was hesitant. His words lacked potency once they fell onto dry paper.

His friends treated her like an older sister and she took to it with the quiet ease of one who chose to love rather than be loved because it was safer. She fed them, watched their games and listened to their confessions. They made her feel wise and protected for the first time in her life. The men grew up with Mickey and she warmed to their loyalty to him. When they came to see her alone, they spoke of him with completeness and affection.

Now they trailed ahead of her and Mickey as the circus filled out its three rings with dancing bears and acrobats and accordion music. Their roaring voices made children's heads turn from the cotton candy and corn dogs. Isabelle laughed with them and took Toddy, the slow-minded one, on her other arm, pointing out to him the elephants with their sashes, the feather-capped horses and the painted clowns. She was the only one outside of his friends who spoke to him as an equal rather than as a child and he always understood her. When she raised her arm, the three silver bracelets that Mickey had given her flew down her arm. They were a present on the second anniversary of their friendship and his face blushed like a boy when he handed her the box, his tall figure stooped with uncharacteristic bashfulness. When she kissed his cheek, he slipped her hands in his, her small narrow fingers stirring like a baby in the cradle of his palm.

They sat looking into the third ring of the circus. A cage was wheeled out and a lion sat staring the crowd with frenzied discontent. "The White Demon!" Someone yelled and the crowd exploded with laughter.

Mickey leaned towards her and repeated, "The White Demon." She looked up to laugh and found his face near hers in a way she had never felt. She suddenly saw he was not as pale as she had always thought and his scent was more lime than musk. He looked down at her so their eyes almost met and she smiled. He reached down and kissed her forehead.

A scream rose like a wave from the middle of the crowd. People began to jump up, fiddling with prizes and purses. People were leaving. Mickey helped Isabelle to her feet.

"What's going on?" She spun around.

Her eyes caught sight of the stage. People surrounded the cage but she could see the door was open. The White Demon was tied down with ropes. The beast was howling with triumph. A child, covered up to her chin with a sheet, was wheeled away, shaking and sobbing. A pool of blood formed near her left shoulder.

The air had become gray and heated as the accordion music played on, reeking of popcorn and tragedy. She felt Mickey's arms around her and heard the voices of his friends speak to her with awkward reassurance. He guided her out of the circus in the echo of ringing bells and accordion music.

In the van, she recovered her voice and, turning to the men, announced, "We're all going to spend the night at Mickey's."

They looked into the mirror, catching their friend's eye. Mickey's lips were a thin line but his eyes were warm. Toddy began to rock and cry. Isabelle turned around and stroked his arm the rest of the way to Mickey's, her bracelets echoing with a tin shiver.

Mickey lived alone in a flat on top of a hill. They set up a communal bed of sleeping bags, blankets, whatever they could find. The living room looked like a canopy of stars without the furniture and lamps. They began to talk quietly about books and movies and the air lifted with their deep voices.

Mickey gave her one of his pajamas and the long arms and cuffs covered her hands and feet. The buttons of the shirt left a gap around her neck. She looked sweet and clownish and Mickey smiled. He tried to make her take his room but she refused, her voice shrill and firm.

"I want to be with all of you," she said. "I trust you."

He realized then how much the injured child had shaken her.

The night was too hot and heavy for the city. Lights in the building across the street flickered with the activity of insomniacs jolted out of bed by the heat. Someone had turned on the radio and it breathed out the soft sounds of a mariachi band. Mickey could see from the fire escape the bee-like movements of neighbors he had never met, and the dark shapes of vases and books.

He rose and wove a silent path around the

sleeping bodies to the kitchen. He began to warm the kettle for tea.

As he watched the steam began to spiral upward, he thought about the four poems he had written that morning on the fire escape as he watched the dawn lift the sun up in its arms. He would throw them away. He had been doing that lately. Not every poem, as there was a poem about the dawn that he liked where he had captured the scents and sounds of the morning. He would show that one to Isabelle. But the other three he could never show her. Their passion was too exhausting.

The door opened and Isabelle, her hair roughed by sleeplessness, leaned against the frame. Her eyes had the bothered expression of one who had been turning something around in her mind for too long.

"I was just – " He looked away.

With a smile, she gently closed the door behind her.

They sat with the tea on the floor, squeezed under the kitchen table because of the intrusion of the dining room furniture. They did not speak.

Isabelle began to sob. She cried in silence, the tears dripping down to the floor. Mickey considered offering up kind words, the kind empty words of one who was far removed from grief. But his lips couldn't move. He reached

14

out and took her hand in his. The bracelets slipped from her wrist and rolled onto the wooden floor with a heavy ring, then lay silent.

They remained holding hands for a while.

Later, a scream in the night woke Isabelle. She could see Toddy's massive figure rocking back and forth a few mattresses away, his face crawling with fear. Mickey was kneeling beside him and speaking in a sweet and gentle voice.

Isabelle stirred, murmuring, "He's afraid the White Demon is going to get him too."

There was silence. The shattering of it disappeared in the black mist of the early morning fog, high over their heads, untouched by the clouds that moved in from the hills.

Mickey's voice rose like a steel wall against a rain of bullets. "No white demon is going to get anyone."

Isabelle laid her head back against the pillow. The softness absorbed her hair, her small head and her lips spreading against the smooth fabric. She felt his warm hand brush against her cheek as he passed her on his way back to bed.

A First Saturday Outing

Helena had not opened a window since she moved into her flat. There was no reason why she shouldn't. There was always a pleasant breeze in San Francisco, so cool and spirited that it made the curtains on the windows float out like the skirt of a doll. She was finally free from her parents whose aging minds made them impossible to deal with during moments of agitation. She was free from her husband and his blank stares that sent her rushing to do the wifely things she somehow always did wrong. She was as liberated as the bird that had been rejected from its flock because of its wild nature.

Buy she had not yet opened a window or gone out. When her divorce came through, she promised herself she would visit the places that interested her and that had been a waste of time for her lethargic parents and pragmatic ex-husband: SF MOMA, The Japanese Tea Garden, Dolores Park. Yet she remained in her flat with the windows closed.

Then she heard about the exhibit of Deenie Brown's lost sculptures at the Walton Museum and dressed for her first outing in a summer suit and straw hat. The city wind was dormant that Saturday. She took the underground train down to Ocean Beach. The museum was hidden between vegetation across from the sand bar in a forlorn corner of the city.

The moment she walked in, Helena was transposed into the one-room schoolhouse. Wooden desks stood between the sculptures and a blackboard showed the shadow of verb conjugations from a lost lesson in the middle of the floor. The windows were boxy and bright and by the time she reached the other side of the exhibit, her eyes were straining from the glare.

Brown's sculptures imposed on the sun enough to hide it inside a patch of clouds. Helena decided to cross the room and then work her way back around the circle to get a closer look at them.

Each sculpture represented a deeper crisis than the previous one, as if the artist had intended to build up to some kind of climax. Each showed a woman, wild-haired and mountainous. Each woman absorbed the look of the one before her and added to it another dimension that was more chilling and complex than the last. A jaw leapt forward, a lip lost faith, and eyes showed the consequence of entrapment.

The exhibition was called *Fumbling Free* and Helena could see why. Entrapment left the women's faces as they thrust their bodies forward, their nakedness protected like shields. The statues near the door stood upright, but as she came to the end of the circle, they crouched and crawled, their bodies smaller as their eyes grew bigger.

The last sculpture showed a tiny woman whose face was made up of eyes. A box with gold rings encircled her like a ball. Helena screeched when she saw it and ran out of the museum.

The woman's face held the same night eyes and her head rolled with the same waves, her body bent in the same fetal position as Helena's when she slept in her bedroom with the door and the window closed.

18

Broken Bows

The red chrome on the Victorian locomotive glared back at the silver trains that stood like angry bullets in the early morning fog. The windows of the Pullman car showed green velvet seats in defiance of the cold white vinyl in the modern cars. Its arches fed into a balcony so that you could imagine the grinning politicians of a back-stabbing era leaning and waving to crowds. The backs of the new trains were smooth and littered with the corpses of dead insects.

To Anne, the refurbished train was a step into a more majestic past. She felt vibrant that she would soon be lost in the moments of another era, one that was less complex and chaotic than her own. She did not regret that she had chosen to take the old masterpiece from Sacramento to Seattle.

She first heard of the train when her mother read her the story about it in the newspaper. Her mother read stories aloud because she expected Anne to laugh or ridicule them just as she did. Her mother had assumed Anne thought and felt the same things she did since Anne was a child.

So she read her the story about a man whose great-grandfather had been an engineer during the steam engine era. The man decided to refurbish one of the old trains with his small inheritance, perhaps the very one his great-grandfather had operated. The story implied there was a reason, a moment of epiphany perhaps, that had led him to the decision, but never gave the details. It was something Anne turned over in her mind even as her mother lamented absurdities.

"Can you imagine?" Her mother had said, putting the paper down to reach for her cigarettes. "So many things he could do with that money. What a waste."

That night, Anne dreamed of the train. Its light gazed down on her like a wise eye and its wheels breathed the steam of progress, blood, and freedom. People stood looking out the train windows outlined in violet like souls without bodies. The whistle blew and steam shot out like a beckoning finger. She ran towards it but something clawed at her body. She smelled the scent of ripened roses, the kind of perfume her mother favored. When the steam cleared, she realized she had made it onto the train. She was surrounded by candles covered with glass bells and she felt surrounded by the warmth of strangers though she could not see them. She woke up with a start but her heart was calm, her hands dry. For days afterwards, every time she thought about the train, she felt the warmth of the covered candles and the strangers.

She ordered her ticket six months in

advance, not because of limited space but because her divorce became finalized then and she was moving to Seattle. Two aging aunts who lived there were well off and needed care. Her mother had arranged it and laid out the rationale one night at a restaurant.

"You're not getting any younger," she said. "You no longer have a husband to take care of you and, at your age, it's unlikely you'll find another one. You have to be taken care of, you know."

"Can't I take care of myself?" Anne had said, folding the linen napkin in her lap into a square.

"That isn't the point," said her mother. "There are family obligations to consider."

Anne knew what she meant. She had been a nurse's aid in her younger days, a good one, before marriage made it unnecessary for her to continue her studies. She had been playing the role of the family life preserver since her teens when she helped to care for her ill father.

"Why shouldn't you save your aunts a little money and find yourself a good situation at the same time?" Her mother said now, sprinkling sugar into her coffee with the care of a diabetic.

"I didn't think it was necessary to find a good situation," Anne had said. "Isn't it enough to just find a happy situation?"

But, of course, her mother convinced her

that no one could just be happy. Everyone needed a good situation and with Anne could find it taking care of people that would take care of her.

Her mother, who had come to see her off, stared at the train with its cat's eye light. "I'll bet it will break down before you cross the Oregon border."

"Of course it won't," said Anne. "Naturally it won't."

"All your savings on this nonsense," she continued. "You have more of your father's waywardness than I realized."

"Dad was never wayward," said Anne. "He never had the chance."

"A plane could get you to Seattle in a few hours at a third of the price," said her mother. "You realize that?"

Anne did not answer at first. She watched spurts of smoke surround the figures that passed her on their way to the compartments.

"Time and money aren't always the most important things, Mom," she said.

"Only someone who can afford to squander them would say that," she snapped.

Anne looked straight at her. "Don't you approve of new experiences?"

"When you're young maybe," she said, putting her arm around her shoulders. "But you're not young."

Anne picked up her small suitcase. "You already said that this morning. Several times."

It seemed an absurd joke now to think that she had tried to explain to her mother the dream of the train, about the people with their inviting smiles and the hope she had felt in its pumping wheels. But her mother hadn't listened. She only fussed about the wrinkled nurse's uniform Anne had not worn for years and went to hunt for the iron.

"It's a waste of time," her mother now said.

"You said that too," said Anne, a little wry. "You know you're repeating yourself, Mom?"

Her mother continued as if she hadn't heard. "A silly whim. An indulgence."

Anne held tight to her purse. At two hundred dollars and large enough to fit three books, her mother called it a silly indulgence too.

"Listen, dear," her mother said. "It isn't too late to give up this idea and take a plane to Seattle."

"But it is," said Anne.

"Nonsense. They said they would accept cancelations until the last minute. I asked them."

Anne glared at her. "I wasn't talking about the money. I told you, some things aren't about money and time."

"And I told *you* - "

Anne pressed her hands against her temples.

She could no longer hear. Her ears were howling as they always did when her mother tried to talk guilt to her. They pierced as if her mother had plunged a stiletto into her forehead so that she couldn't see or think.

"Goodbye, Mom."

She turned away from her now so that she wouldn't have to look at the grainy face and eyes. Her ears stopped howling and she felt safe again.

As she followed the other passengers, a hard wind wrapped white smoke around her, holding her up like the arms of a warm giant.

The porter struggled to raise the leather case with her books through the narrow doorway. She felt embarrassed by its size.

"Maybe it should go in the baggage car," she suggested.

A boy with a head of short waves bent down and pulled it up from the inside. When she smiled her thank you, she realized he was not a boy at all but a man and not exactly a young one. His angular face, pale lips, and grey eyes told of past exuberance that had now fallen in shadows.

The man left an imprint in her mind as the strangers of her dream, hidden in the shadows of the covered candles.

She learned more about him, quite by accident, from a woman named Bea who was taking the trip with her granddaughter Carla. As Bea flipped through magazines with glossy covers of happy families, she chatted on and off, telling Anne that the grey-eyed man she had seen was a musician. The man's name was Blaze Colt and he was well into his forties. He was a violinist who had played Carnegie Hall when he was just twelve. At fifteen, he was invited back and played with such a passion that he broke a bow during his performance. Thereafter, he made a show of breaking bows. But in the last year, he had become, in Bea's words, "a bit of a sinker".

"What do you mean?" asked Anne.

"We saw a concert of his a few years ago," said Carla. She took one of the cocktail napkins and dabbed her wrist. "Nothing wrong with it but nothing right either."

They invited her to play a game of cards but Anne declined. She had begun to feel queasy from the motion of the train so she stepped out into the walkway where someone had opened a window. Leaning against the wall, she closed her eyes and breathed in the magnificent air. When she opened them, a picture frame of a man's profile, a man with wavy hair, faced her from the opposite compartment.

*

Blaze sat on the leather chair in the smoking lounge with one hand holding the cigarette he had barely touched. The other was curled into a fist that propped up his face. His jaw was wired tight, his eyes ironed with observation. His father had taught him that someone was always watching and he must always be on the defense. These last years, that someone was a demon his father had named Lucas, a demon that became the ruin of his balance and his reason.

His father was convinced that Lucas could split in two, one half making deviltry for the father and the other chasing the son. Lucas was his explanation for why Blaze's talent had collapsed.

The train went into a tunnel. The darkness brought on the melancholy he had been protesting in his music since he was a teenager. It folded over him like the lid of a coffin. His breathing became heavy and blank. But then, the train passed through the tunnel and he was all right again, taking in dust and nicotine. He pressed his lips against his hand. The words of a young musician at his last concert came back to him: *Fight the lost passion. You began with broken bows, now end with them.*

He had been feeling for a while that he was swept up into a funnel. Like Alice, he found the rabbit hole but it didn't lead to a fairytale Wonderland. As far as he could see, it led nowhere.

As he ambled out of the smoking lounge, he passed by Anne. But she was such a tiny shadow that he didn't notice her.

*

That evening, Anne sat with Bea and Carla in the dining car. Ten minutes in, she began to feel the heaviness of the cushioned walls and enclosed space. The chandelier hanging in the center of the car swung back and forth like a pendulum and her earlier dizziness returned.

"How can the rest of the train be so wide and this car so oppressive?" Anne couldn't help but lament.

"Must be the heat," said Carla. "The steam from the hot plates gets into the air and stays there. Don't laugh, Gran, it's true!"

As the two were arguing the point, Blaze stepped into the dining car. He was loosely dressed and walked with the wiry step of one who had been trying to sleep for a while but without success. He sat in the corner nearest to the door.

"All done in," said Bea, eyeing him.

"I suppose we should feel sorry for him," said Carla, buttering a slice of bread.

"I don't!"

Anne gave at Bea a sharp look. The woman's eyes were pointed now that she had finished ordering and put away her reading glasses.

27

"Why not?" she ventured.

"Because Gran thinks he as good as killed his college roommate, that's why," Carla said. "Gran doesn't take a compassionate view of such things."

Anne looked towards the corner table. The man's dark eyes had lifted to the ceiling with an alarming concentration.

""He looks hardly capable of it," she said.

"Oh, not literally," said Bea. "He didn't take a gun to the boy's head. It was the competition. You know how those performing arts colleges are. All that throat cutting. They say that Blaze Colt would have crossed the line in those days. He was intense then. Not the musty thing you see now."

"It was his father's fault, Gran," said Carla. "Now *there* was a heartless bastard, they said."

"Dear, please," Bea hissed.

"Well, you said it yourself," said the granddaughter, moving the bread aside to make room as the server set the roast chicken down. "Pushed and pushed. He even had a professional violinist record a piece of music and send it to the college admissions board in Blaze's name. Imagine, he was breaking bows since he was a teenager but his father didn't trust him to get into college on his own."

Anne stared openly at the man. He had not touched the food in front of him, had not even looked at it. His eyes were still on the ceiling. She had the obscene thought that he was praying, his fearful eyes towards God.

"And the roommate?" she asked.

"I expect the young man couldn't handle the pressure," said Carla. "So he killed himself. Hung himself by a rope."

"He was driven to it," Bea insisted. "Those who are pushed, push others. Like the child who watches his father drink becomes a drunk himself."

"Really, Gran!"

"He found the body, didn't he?" she said, her voice snapping cold in the heavy room. "That's proof enough. He found the body."

"That proves nothing," said Carla.

Anne could no longer hear their squabbling. Blaze's eyes were transparent. He rose, still looking at the ceiling and walked out of the dining car without having eaten a bite.

When they left, Anne lingered for a moment near the door. She realized that Blaze had been looking at the rocking chandelier.

*

The next morning the train flew through the grey desert. Blaze watched it passing by through the window. The cactus was brown and parched and birds circled in the grey sky. It was as if the desert were recovering from some bloody battle where no one had won.

He thought about the last year his father had fallen ill. The doctor thought it was a virus but his father knew it was the beginnings of a madness that would eventually consume him.

"No virus ever caused insanity," Blaze objected.

"There is no telling what Lucas will do," his father answered, his eyes white. Emaciated with delusions, his father's eyes had turned milky and smooth. Those were the eyes that glared at him like an image in a mirror when he rehearsed or sat alone in the hotel room after it had emptied of well-wishers. He had almost convinced himself it was a figment of his tired mind.

It was the same reality his father had denied when he heard Blaze play the piece that belonged to Nechamah. He was nineteen and his father had forbidden him to ever play it again.

"You'll be chasing disaster if you do," he had said. For his father, anything less lively than Vivaldi or Mozart was disaster. Even Chopin with his falling stars and his love sickness was too maudlin for audiences.

Blaze took the music out of the inner pocket of his violin case. The pages were smooth and white but the grey light of the desert made them rough like granite.

He played, his bow sounding each note with

care. The slowness of it was what had irked his father. Each note was a footstep, a sob, a gasp. One did not obliterate another, nor did any fly or leap or laugh. The notes flew out of the arms of a dream and into a nightmare.

Those had been Pid's words. Pid, his roommate and friend, had listened in silence when he played it for him, a cigarette in his mouth and his index finger pressed to his chin. When it was over, he grabbed one of his art books and showed Blaze Fuseli's painting *The Nightmare*, with the woolly demon sitting on the woman in white tulle. He said, in a strange mixture of envy and triumph, "You recreated him in music." Pid was always trying to make some face in a painting come alive on his piano.

Blaze finished the piece and laid his hand heavy on the bow. Someone sighed behind him and he turned to see a woman standing outside the door to his compartment. Through the frosted glass he could not see her face clearly but her figure looked almost impish. He slid open the door. It was the woman he had helped with her suitcase the day before.

Her smile now was warm and disarming.

"It doesn't sing much, does it?" He said.

"Sing?"

"The music."

"It sings another tune." Her hand clasped the

wooden doorframe.

"You mean a howling tune," he said sharply.

The woman leaned one hand on top of the velvet seat. "Who wrote it?"

He thought about telling her the story of Nechamah in the way he told it to his father, a logical story of discovering the piece and honoring it after researching it to find out it was written in a death camp, a tune to defy burned bones and flesh. But looking at her serene face, it would be a disgrace to lie to her, a contribution to evil. One of Lucas' pranks.

So he told her the truth. "I wrote it."

She slid onto the velvet cushion. "For a dead boy."

He dropped to his knees on the carpeted floor, the violin collapsing at his feet. "How did you know?"

"Tell me."

There was something about her manner that reminded him of a glass woman his mother had always loved. The woman stood with her arms outstretched, sashes floating alongside her body so that it looked as if she carried wings. His mother was clutching the statuette when she died and he convinced his father to bury it with her. Although this woman did not have wings, he could almost feel the warmth of outstretched arms.

He told her about Pid and the tiny apartment

they had rented off campus. He told her about their drunken duets with him at the violin and Pid at the piano, playing jazz and rock, laughing at how his father and Pid's mother would had lectured them about the inferiority of popular music. He told her about Pid's pills, his pacing and his hands that shook all through their last year and wouldn't stop. And then he told her about the rope, frayed from holding together the trunk that had belonged to his great-grandfather that his father had given him for luck, the rope that had seen Paris, Venice, Singapore, Athens. The rope Pid wasn't supposed to find.

They were silent for a time. She was now on the floor beside him, her legs folded under her. The dense carpet exhaled her lily perfume.

"Nobody knows that it's yours?"

"Not the one I wanted to know."

He looked down at her hands that had taken his own. They were troubled hands. Not the hands of a glass angel.

"What's the name of it?" she asked.

"Dignity Of The Dead," he said.

"Why play it now?" She asked. "For the dead boy?"

"For a dead man," he said. "No. For two dead and one dying."

His face dropped in his hands.

He felt her touch on his shoulder. There was

something sweet about it, something that shot a spark through his body. It was the same spark that had rocked him when he had first played the music on the balcony, before he knew that his father was watching.

He thought he heard her say, "Playing a different tune is like Lazarus rising from the ashes."

He raised his head to answer but found he was alone in his compartment.

*

Two days later, Anne met the aunts and the temporary nurse whom she was to replace at the train station in Seattle. Their sallow skin and spotted necks told her they had already settled into their long illness. As she was helping one aunt into the car, she heard the faint notes of a violin singing tears across the quiet parking lot. Her spine rang with it, but it was not the deadness of bone but something indefinable and alive. The notes played the steps of one Lazarus and one Lady Lazarus.

Gnarled Bones

"Let Love clasp Grief lest both be drown'd" –
Alfred Lord Tennyson, "In Memoriam A.H.H"

Em and Denny were seven and thirteen when their parents died. They died in a crowd, their eyes glaring around them for the devil they had always told their children would destroy them if they didn't keep silent and hidden. The house they built on the outskirts of Muir Woods was almost a fortress surrounded by redwoods and a lake spilling almost into the backyard. But the children didn't mind. The geese and piping loons were their companions and their parents stayed home, teaching them from antiquated books. Once a horn sounded from the crooked road that led out to town, a car that had gotten lost. The glass-eyed glare from Em and Denny's parents made the driver leave thick tire tracks in the dirt as he sped away.

The only two people their parents trusted were Emmanuel, the gardener and grounds keeper, and Lupe, his wife, who tended the house while their mother alternated between teaching them from the old books and sleeping in her room, wrapped in the pain of her migraine headaches. Their parents cast Emmanuel and Lupe as protectors of their children, believing in a world that shattered any illusion of finding happiness or sanity that they didn't want Em or Denny to endure alone.

When the parents died, Emmanuel and Lupe were given temporary custody of the children until their permanent guardian, a godmother named Goldie, could be found. Left to their own devices, the children's silence was like a constant droning above the hushed voices of the Mexican couple and the sweeping wind. People who had known their parents before their paranoiac days were familiar with the children only as far as a Saturday casserole or a Sunday roast could take them. Lupe would smile and lean into the door, blocking any further entrance. The Mexican couple hid the children as much as possible when the social workers darted through the house like dust snapping out of a rug, asking questions and making notes. In those months before Goldie took them into the city, Em and Denny existed in a nullified world of books and fajita dinners that the gardener's wife served them in paper plates.

The Mexican couple had been used to mild conversations between the children when their parents were alive. Now it was as if their parents had taken their children's tongues with them to their grave. Emmanuel and Lupe heard barely a syllable coming out of their mouths when they were in the room with the children.

Em and Denny's eyes would converse as they sat with books spread on the floor between them. They read silently the words of Byron and Dickinson. They hummed the nursery rhymes that their mother used to sing to them to bring silence into the night. The couple could hear the humming but not the words.

Emmanuel and Lupe sometimes talked softy among themselves, speculating how the children's voices came out at night when they had retired to the bowels of the house. Lupe would sometimes peep down the hall at the two rooms joined by a single wall. She could just make out the children sitting up in bed. They were awake, staring at one another through the wall with blank eyes.

Once Lupe, turning away from the glass, thought she saw Em's blurry eyes lift and her brother, in return, kick out his chin. But Emmanuel convinced her that what she had seen was only the tree limbs outside playing with the light. Not a word was spoken, so how could there be acknowledgement?

The social workers finally found Goldie, the widowed godmother, living in a small town near Lake Tahoe. Goldie quickly sold the fortress and bought a small but adept house in the Mission district in San Francisco where the streets streamed with colored paper and lights during the Spanish holidays and schools were close by. The Mexican couple willingly gave up their guardianship with relieved smiles. This godmother, they agreed, would bring them out of their silent madness.

*

May 10, 1990

Today marks five years since we've been with Goldie. She made us fudge cake and opened a bottle of champagne for herself and a little for Denny. Denny joked about how we must have driven her to become a closeted smoker because when she leaned forward to kiss him, he could smell nicotine on her collar. She told us the story of how she had chain smoked to steady her patience with drunken gamblers and her husband when he gave her lame excuses as to why he was always letting their money run out of the small casino they ran on the Nevada side of Tahoe.

Denny says she has control of most of our money but she's using little of it for herself even though she loves buying things with velvet and lace trimmings. Denny begged her to keep Emmanuel on and she hired Lupe as a full-time housekeeper, although I don't see that we need her. Goldie is enough of a watcher, running after me, sweeping up after my experiments with the flower pots and making sure Denny's clothes are clean and his face shaven.

She said she cried the whole night after Denny threw his backpack in the dumpster after he finished high school, saying he'd do better educating himself, though she never said a word about it at the time. Maybe that's why she forces me to sit down with them when Denny reads in the garden. But I don't mind. I love the funny way she has of talking about American heroes, as if they were the hot dog vendors on Market Street, chiding them like a preschool teacher.

Denny's been complaining lately that our lives are meaningless. I'm happy keeping to my flowers, haggling with the prune-faced women on Mission Street for the best azaleas and lilies. I can spend a whole afternoon reading about flowers and arranging them in glass vases. But Denny is too restless and roams all day to who the hell knows where. He comes home with the dust of cigarette ash that doesn't belong to him, smelling of gin or beer. His kisses are always sweet, though. Where does he get all those rose-scented notes with embroidered initials like O.P, C.D, and B.C? He never brings any girl home and he ignores the women who try to catch his brass-colored eye on our weekend walks. He promised me that Sundays at Golden Gate Park belong to me and no one else and he always keeps his promises. We fall into the silence of our childhood when we walk alone. I don't know why.

*

One night, Denny came in late to dinner with a bunch of unlit cigarettes in the pocket of his jacket. He took a sliver of toast slippery with olive oil and picked at the crust of Parmesan before he dropped it in a plate with a clang.

"Em, you should think about marrying Tommy."

His sister, angry at the way his eyes were damp from cigarette smoke and rose perfume, threw an olive pit at him.

"He is a nice boy, Em." Goldie said.

"Maybe that's the trouble," said Denny. "He's a *boy*."

"A brute, you mean." Em said.

"He's not a brute and you know it." Goldie's chiding voice sounded dim.

"You're disintegrating in this house alone." He sat down. "We all are. A husband might at least give us something to fight about."

His voice bounced with anticipation. He liked anything new, like books he could exchange for new ones at the used book stores, dishes with packing peanuts still stuck to them, colored vases for Em, satin pin cushions for Goldie. Em wondered if Denny sought out the ash and rose-scented notes because they promised something that could rise and begin again.

"Let's go do something, then," Em said.

He ran his hand through his hair. He had gotten highlights just that week. "Such as?"

"Something wholesome and old-fashioned." She leaned into the table. "Rent some bikes and ride into Muir Woods or go see the bears at the Oakland Zoo or–" But he was laughing.

"For God's sake, Em, you're no longer children," Goldie sighed.

"As if that has anything to do with it!"

Denny brushed his lips against her cheek and then Goldie's. He slid a cigarette out of his pocket. Em smelled the mint tightly bound inside the heady tobacco.

"Tommy was asking about you, that's all."

He was gone, his dinner cold and untouched. The women finished their meal in deliberate silence as if a corpse lay in the other room and they were wary of disturbing it.

*

May 23, 1990

We found out today that one of Denny's lungs is weak. Dr. Finestone was vague about it but warned, no more cigarettes and no more rose-scented notes. He keeps going out anyway despite Goldie's reprimands. He sits by my bed when he comes home to talk but after he's gone, I go over the conversation in my head and realize what he really said was nothing at all. No more silent speech and no more humming between walls for us. I miss that. We used to pour our hearts out to each other. Denny says all that is childish now. He seems to think everything I love is childish.

Tommy doesn't think I'm a child. He likes it that I take his birds seriously. He has chickens and ducks and a pelican some fisherman takes care of for him on the pier. He has eyes like a snake's but he's not quite as boorish as I first thought. Goldie says his mother has a chest full of family jewels and no daughters of her own. As if I'd give a damn about that.

Tommy took me to the pier to see his pelican the other day. It's the stiffest thing I ever saw, eyeing people as they walk by with their fried shrimp and clams. It seemed to warm a little once Tommy coaxed its beak open with a few sardines. Then he showed me how to fish. When I actually caught one, I insisted he throw it back. He just laughed in that plucky way of his, like Denny when he catches on to a joke. I like that in him.

*

"What do you think of aunts, Em?" Denny said one evening.

"Whose?" His sister brushed back a lock of thread from behind the cross-stitched picture. She had started learning the craft a few weeks ago.

"Ours, of course."

Goldie looked up from her book. "What on earth are you talking about?"

"I think we should get ourselves an aunt."

He said it as easily as he would say that they should ask Lupe to make baklava for dessert.

Goldie grabbed the coffee spoon about to fall out of her cup. By her trembling fingers, Em knew he had offended their godmother.

But Denny was as perceptive as he was blunt. He put his arms around Goldie. "It has nothing to do with you, darling. You know no one could ever take your place." His eyes melted the sting and she smiled.

"A godmother isn't enough anymore," he continued.

"It's better with just us," said Em.

"Don't be so narrow-minded." His foot tapped against her ankle. "An aunt will give you someone to take care of."

His sister glared at him. "Now who's being narrow-minded?" She eyed Goldie, looking for support. But the woman had gone back to her book.

"She has to be young," Denny said. "Young and anxious with red curls."

"Why anxious?" Em said.

He grinned. "Don't be daft, Em. We have all the trimmings, don't we?"

She closed her eyes. Denny's circular talk

43

made her dizzy. His words could go round and round like a broken carousel.

"Soothing an anxious young aunt," he mused, stirring his tea with a cinnamon stick. "Some unfortunate woman is bound to need us."

"You mean some poor dirty woman living down on Market Street?" she said.

"Not poor and dirty. Forgotten."

"He's playing games, dear," Goldie said. "Don't let it frighten you." Her thin hands warmed a spot of her bones.

"Youth and aunts don't always go together," said Em.

"You're an insult to anyone's imagination," he said, tossing his arm back over the chair.

"Goldie, tell him he's crazy!"

A vibration filled the room and the windows rattled as if an earthquake were rumbling through the city. But it was only their cat Fielding thumping across the wooden floor to settle near Denny's feet.

"Christ, Goldie, for once let him hear the truth!"

Their godmother lifted her head and her eyes were uncertain. But then her gaze melted. It wasn't adoration, although Denny was always the first to get that. They settled with finality. The decision was made, though not blindly.

*

44

June 5, 1990

Denny's been away for three days now. I rattle around the house like the wind, but Goldie insists he is a grown man and therefore not lost. But I know she's just as worried as I am. She moves in slow motion and her feet are unsteady with each step. Lupe consoles us in Spanish and even though we don't understand a syllable, we feel protected.

I checked with the hospital where Dr. Finestone did all the tests but Denny hasn't set foot in there for a while. Goldie said it's absurd to think that Denny wouldn't tell us if he were sick. I don't see how those grey walls could ever hold Denny even if he did get sick. When we were kids, one of our stories was about the Rainbow Boy who had pneumonia and was so terrified by his confinement that he colored all his walls with crayons. They found him suffocated in the morning. But Denny wouldn't allow them to lock him up that way.

Tommy's been roaming the streets in his father's van all day looking for him but no one has seen Denny. His mother came by with roasted turkey and rhubarb pie. Mrs. Rhodes called Denny the wandering Boy Blue and laughed. I had to remind her he wasn't a boy anymore.

*

On the forth day of his absence, when a

storm had blown the dust across the windows, a message arrived from Denny. Goldie was to bake a cherry cobbler and he would bring home the ice cream. He wanted Em to make a daisy bouquet - one for the dining room table and one for the corner bedroom that was to be Aunt Priscilla's. Lupe was to make ginger snaps because Aunt Priscilla liked ginger. He finished off with a word to Em about getting the antique dolls out of the attic so Aunt Priscilla could look at them.

Em crushed the note and threw it into the trash. Aunt Priscilla was a stranger but already she was the center of the household.

At least she wasn't poor or dirty. Em could see that as they sat through dinner, the dining room polished like the face of a penny and the china slippery under salmon oil and hollandaise sauce.

"Priscilla – "

But she was interrupted by the woman's milky voice. "Call me Aunt Penny, please!"

"Priscilla," Em continued, bearing her brother's glare. "Are you from the city?"

The woman turned her lamb's face to Denny, waiting for a signal.

"Are you somebody's sister or stepmother?" She continued. Goldie's foot dug into her ankle.

Through the rest of dinner, she tried to catch the woman's eye. But she could not fit the lively voice of the little woman to any of the rose-scented notes.

After dinner, they sat in the living room and inspected the dolls. Denny's chatter soon got on Em's nerves. Evenings like this when the dust scraping against the glass, he usually sat back and watched her and Goldie play cards with a contented smile. But for an hour now, his voice had been grating on like a creaky gate, his chin damp with sweat and his eyes animated.

"You sound like one of those street vendors," Em remarked. "Trying to sell your soggy hotdogs."

"Be kind, Em." Goldie's hissed.

"She can't, Goldie." Denny said. "She's forgotten the meaning of the word."

His voice lifted taut in the quiet room. The love that Em was used to was gone. His hands no longer moved gently into hers. One hand now held up a doll by her hair and the other threaded around Priscilla's elbow.

"Don't fight!" Priscilla said. The delight of being surrounded by a quartet of china dolls faded. "There will never be an end to it if you do."

Em glared at the woman folded on the velvet couch like a corkscrew. She was oozing blood red curls and pale anxious skin. Her head bobbed from one person to another as her eyes zipped between them. She asked questions with a morbid curiosity which both she and Denny had despised as children.

"Denny and I never fight."

Goldie leaned forward. "You've never been such a brat before."

The words stung. Goldie was their whole-hearted savior who had had the courage to take care of them when they were abandoned and thrust out into the world devout of happiness and sanity. Dear Goldie, with her thin hands and her sweet smile, calling her a brat.

The red curls shriveled like petals from a shaking rose. Priscilla's youngish face, pale as a spirit, became subdued. The child in her dissolved into a worn woman.

"I don't think Em is a brat. Just very young."

Priscilla's coarse eyes threw aside the moonlight as she scrutinized Em. A meddling mouse, Em was sure. Her eager little hands thrust forward, her fingers twirling like twigs.

"It's that poetry she reads," said Denny. "Poetry darkens the mind."

But the next day, he came home with a box full of books from the poets for Priscilla. She said she was intrigued by the passion with which they scrawled their fervent phrases. He would not allow Em to read them.

"I'm sure I'll appreciate them more than Priscilla," she insisted.

Folds appeared near Priscilla's eyes and

wariness settled on her face.

"Don't cause a commotion, Em," Denny said.

Em eyed the woman. "Have *you* ever caused a commotion, Priscilla?"

"Shut up, Em," Denny snapped but the glance from the adopted aunt made him turn away and concentrate on the brandy he had poured himself.

"I don't know," she said. "What do you consider a commotion?" She peered at the glass paintings of fish on the opposite wall.

"Protest, of course," said Em.

"Against what?"

"God, anything!"

Priscilla leaned against the back of a disheveled desk, holding one of the dolls to her chest. "I don't have your courage."

Em stared at her, feeling sick.

Denny led Priscilla to bed, leaving her alone with a tin echo of their footsteps. Bitter tears filled her eyes, stinging and dry like parchment. There would be no floating conversations between her and Denny tonight.

*

March 19, 1991:

Denny's had a fever for a week now. When I try to bring him jellybeans and newspapers, Goldie snaps at me that I agitate his nerves. But Priscilla can push all the furry knitted scarves and socks at him that she wants and Goldie just nods. I hate seeing how infantile he's become with Priscilla, pressing his forehead against her shoulder and asking her to tuck the blanket around him even though he looks like a body prepared for burial.

Now he's insisting that I look after Priscilla while he's sick. Look after her? She's taken over the house. I can't get away from her goldfish eyes, those two fleshy marbles. The rest of her is so prickly but not those eyes. She's really not so innocent after all. She still won't tell me how old she is.

And he keeps sending me messages through Priscilla. Today, she came into my room without knocking, perching herself on the bed like a sailboat, her round chin in her hands. Then, she said, "Denny wants you to marry Tommy."

"He told you that?"

"He told me that."

She was lying. I know she was lying. I could see by the way her eyes shifted to the edge of the bedspread, spearing one of the pompoms with her sharp little hand. She just wants me to think that she and Denny speak through silence, that they understand each other. But Denny won't speak in silence with anyone but me.

*

March 22, 1991:

Priscilla and I spent most of the day strolling around the garden because Denny is in the hospital again. What a useless endeavor! Beginning on one side of the garden and then ending at the same point under the apple tree.

But Denny made me her watchdog until the doctors can stabilize his lungs, so we stroll. I'm sure Goldie would have dragged the woman with her on her chores but she loathes interference. She once told us that when we get married, we should plan around her. The way she said it, wiping diamonds of sweat off her face with a handkerchief, made Denny laugh. He asked her if she had a thousand godchildren that she should be so wary of weddings. It was one of the few times I've ever seen Goldie really angry with him.

Now a strange nurse tends to Denny every morning unless Goldie can make it out to the hospital on the six a.m. bus. The nurse rattles on about outside germs and tries to keep people away. Goldie believes her nonsense so I'm not allowed to visit Denny. But on quiet afternoons when the heat scurries up the windows like a mole, I sneak out of the house and go to the hospital. Once I found a candy cane uniform and put it on so that I could get a peek inside his room. His body was matted behind a mesh tent and I couldn't see the pearl cheeks I wanted so much to kiss. I think a kiss would have brought him home. I'm sure of it.

*

Em spent the next week needling news of Denny's progress out of Priscilla. Despite Goldie's disapproval, Priscilla didn't hold back the graphic details of his bloody coughs, wheezing breath, and sighs. Em curled up in the blankets at night and tried not to look at the wall that separated her from Denny's empty room. She was still not allowed to see him, but Priscilla could visit whenever she wanted. Goldie insisted this was because Priscilla was older and knew more about healthcare, as she had nursed her husband through a long illness. Em didn't say that she knew only the kiss of a sister would bring him home.

One night, left alone with Priscilla for dinner while Goldie was at the hospital, the woman suddenly asked her about Tommy.

She picked at the edges of the slimy grilled cheese. "I think he's going to ask me to marry him soon."

Priscilla's face turned sour as she gave her the usual worn look. Em didn't know what she loathed more, the woman's goosey giggle or the gnarly old maid look.

She patted her wrist like a meager puppet. "Maybe he won't."

"You sound almost hopeful."

"Marriage is not easy," she said. She laid

52

down her fork.

"I know that." Em said. "Did you think I thought it was easy?"

"You're a willful girl, Em," she said, peering up at her with a dim glow.

"Denny likes me that way."

"Don't you think you should wait until Denny gets better so you can consult him?"

"I thought you said that he told you he wanted me to marry Tommy."

"I lied."

Em could not help but smile with the feeling of righteousness. She rose from the table.

"He needs you now," said Priscilla. "You do know that, don't you?"

Em retreated to her room in a rage. She realized Priscilla wouldn't have said such a thing unless she got it from Denny. So she had been lying before but now she wasn't. She had spoken to Denny and he told her to say that he needed her. Needed her but not enough to demand her healing kisses, her hand pressed against his to make him strong again. He had to send this sulfurous mouse as his messenger.

*

April 3, 1991:

My eyes are tired. I've been reading Wordsworth all day. He looks more barbaric than his poetry lets on, all that barbed wire curling around his face so that you can't even see his lips. Maybe Denny and Tommy have spoiled me with their boyish charms. Other women can't stand it but why should I mind? You don't have to fake seriousness with a boy.

Priscilla came into the living room while I was reading. She almost never sits there during the day because the sun hurts her eyes. She's not looking well at all.

She dusted off a chair and gave me in a vague smile.

"I miss Denny," she said in a sniveling way.

"I don't see why. You visit him all the time," I said. I should have been kinder, I know, but her griping gets on my nerves. I don't know how Denny can stand it, but I think sometimes he really sees himself as some lost hero, like in the operettas he used to listen to.

"Read to me, Em," she said.

"Denny will be home soon to read to you," I said. "And stroll with you and play with you like a little boy."

"I had a boy," she said in a quiet voice. "He wasn't anything like Denny."

Her eyes grew molten and her jaw slackened. The knitting she dragged around with her was dusty as if it had been sitting on the ground for days. She looked as if she hadn't had a decent night's sleep since Denny's illness.

"Can I get you some coffee?"

"What?" She gave me a bumbling look.

"Maybe you should go lie down, Priscilla."

God, why did I have to do Goldie's job? But Goldie hardly gives me her hugs and petting anymore. She's too preoccupied with Denny, her rousing fair boy. I've been ejected from the family, from everyone but Denny. That's the way it's always been.

Priscilla's hands lay inside mine. They were sinewy, gnarly things. Odd that her hands show the age that's been drained from her face.

"Read to me," she said, "Please, Em."

I was trapped by her broken voice like when she and Denny used to take their walks around the house. Between the silences, she would begin sentences and then trail off: "That tree reminds me of – " "That last storm we had – ". She would speak in that same voice and her words were eaten up by dust.

*

April 11, 1991:

Denny's still in the hospital and the doctors say it will be a while before he can come home. No one will tell me anything and they caught me the last time I sneaked into his room in the candy cane pinafore. So now I can't get closer than the nurse's station before I'm shuffled out.

But this morning, Goldie let me come with her to the hospital. The nurse helped him raise his head. He looked so weak, poor darling Denny! Goldie said no, but I flew to him. He whispered that my kisses energized him like wild strawberries fizzing in the sun. Goldie says he couldn't possibly have said a thing since his illness makes him too breathless to speak a complete sentence. She doesn't know it, but I had a whole silent conversation with him in those few minutes I saw him about Priscilla and Tommy and his birds and the bouquets I put in his room every morning. I know he understood me because his hand curved around mine.

*

April 19, 1991:

Goldie stays in the hospital all day now, so Priscilla is in charge of the household. I like her better when she's sitting with her knitting untouched in her lap, her face staring out the window with that gnarly look on it. Now she spends most of the day roaming the house and the garden, picking flowers that I later find abandoned all over the house. She pushed Lupe to her limit today by almost ripping her apron off of her waist. "Rest, rest!" she shouted at her with one gnarled little finger pointing at her like a cross. "Out the door, out, out!" And wouldn't you know it, Priscilla made us all dinner. Potato soup, something she called Devil's Stew, and bread pudding swimming in butter. I do believe she's practicing for when Denny gets home. She seems to think the hospital stay will end with that.

Goldie comes home every night dragging the basket of food back with her untouched, her face coarse and blank. He still has the mesh tent around him and his skin is grey like a dove's. She won't tell me anything else but sometimes I steal away from under Lupe's eye and find the window of his hospital room and peer in. That's only happened a few times because Lupe has taken it into her head to play keeper on me like she did when I was a child. I think she still sees me as the tiny leopard I was when she first met me and she's preparing for when I will fall into her arms, when Denny dies. Tommy's been sending me feathers from his birds in pink envelopes. He never includes a note, but I know it's him. They smell of bleach and I wonder if he had the fisherman's wife wash them for me. There is something so delicate and clean about them.

*

April 28, 1991

I understand now about Priscilla's hands. Grief makes gnarly bones. They are mine now.

Denny never made it out of the hospital. I think I knew it would come, even when I refused to believe.

Goldie won't let me wear a veil.

"You're his sister," she said. "Not his widow."

Priscilla is crying all the time. "He wanted joy, that's all he ever wanted," she sobs. "Don't you think, looking down from Heaven – "

Heaven. Denny never mentioned Heaven and I won't either.

They don't know. The day Denny died, I stole away to the hospital. They were wiping his face in the hospital morgue, the Mole Hole, I heard the interns refer to it. I slipped in when they were gone and put my cheek against his. It was still warm like when he was flushed after telling me his silent stories. I close my eyes and I can still hear the stories about Mattie the Turtle and Potato Boy who was forced to work in the fields and sang at the top of his lungs Alive, Alive, Alive. They think that locking Denny up in a wooden box can keep him from telling me stories. What do they know?

*

May 8, 1991

I spent the whole day looking at the toys we brought with us from the old house. Denny's tin soldiers felt like ice sculptures as I held them. His favorite stuffed animal Lucifer scowled at me. Even though it was filthy with dust, the mule could still look evil with his button eyes. The rocking horse, the wooden boatmen, everything rejected me. *Intruder*, their hollow lips scream. I lay on the floor and cried. But there is no Denny to kiss the tears away before they wash my face like rainwater.

The house is a cave of echoes and walls. We barely speak. Only our footsteps chant until we go to bed. Priscilla seems to hear nothing. Her face is just one long blank stare.

Yesterday, she scared me. I was looking for the poem by Yeats that Denny used to love, the one about Leda and the swan. I hear him reading the violent verse backwards so that it's Leda who triumphs, clipping the swan's wings.

Priscilla was hiding like an owl behind the curtain. I saw her hands first. They were grey as if she had plunged them in a mercury bath. Not dove grey like Denny's cheeks but odd silver hands.

I ran into Goldie's room. It had the sharp scent of rose water.

"You said if any of us got married, we should plan around you," I said.

She looked dazed for a moment.

"I'm going to marry Tommy."

She folded her arms around her and cried.

In spite of myself, I found my arms twisted around her, wringing away at the flesh on her shoulders. "Don't, Goldie. Denny wanted it. Didn't he?"

She peered up at my face with the sweet smile. It was the way she had looked at me and Denny the first time she saw us after our parents died.

ACKNOWLEDGEMENTS

I'd like to thank the following people:
Dr. Jackie Kolosov of Texas Tech University,
English Department, for her patience and feedback
on my story, "Gnarled Bones".

The Women Fiction Writer's Association (WFWA)
for their dedication to encouraging and supporting
women writers.

To my WFWA critique group whose honest and
insightful feedback helped me see my writing and
myself as a writer in a new light.

ABOUT THE AUTHOR

Tam May was born in Israel and moved to the United States when she was a baby. She grew up in the States and went back to Israel to finish high school and earn her college degree in English Literature and Linguistics before she returned to the States, where she currently resides. She started writing when she was 14 and writing became her voice. She writes psychological fiction that explores emotional realities informed by personal and collective past experience, dreams, emotions, fantasies, nightmares, imagination, and self-analysis. She is especially fascinated by how our personal past informs the present and the demons that we carry within ourselves and eventually overcome even as they leave their imprint behind. She believes the past informs how we think, feel, and act and coming to terms with these demons changes the future.

Tam May can be found on:
WEBSITE: www.tammayauthor.com
BLOG: https://thedreambook.wordpress.com/
EMAIL: tammay70@tammayauthor.com
FACEBOOK: https://www.facebook.com/tammayauthor/
TWITTER: https://twitter.com/tammayauthor

OTHER BOOKS BY TAM MAY

Coming in 2018

THE ORDER OF ACTAEON (WAXWOOD
NOVELLA SERIES: BOOK 1)

Sometimes the hunter becomes the hunted.

Jake is the heir of the prominent Alderdice family in
San Francisco. Although dearly loved by his sister
Vivian, his love of art and his static life have made
him a pariah in the eyes of his tyrannical mother
Larissa.

When the Alderdices take their yearly summer
vacation in the prominent resort town of Waxwood,
Jake meets Stevens, an older man who lives up to
Larissa's ideals of manhood with his paternal
authority and his obsession for power and
leadership. He develops a hero worship for Stevens,
who in turn is intrigued by Jake's artistic talent.
Stevens introduces him to The Order Of Actaeon, a
group of misanthropes who have rejected the
commercial and conventional luxuries of their
former lives for a "pure" life in the wild.

But behind the potent charms of his new friend and
the seductive simplicity of the Order's lifestyle lies
something brutal and sinister that Jake could not

have anticipated.

Coming soon

THE CLAUSTROPHOBIC HEART (WAXWOOD
NOVELLA SERIES: BOOK 2)

*Sometimes maternal love can damage the object of
its affection.*

Gena Flax has been devoted to her Aunt Helen since
her mother died when she was ten. She denies that
Helen's clinging and irrational jealousies could be
anything more than maternal affection because of
her loyalty and gratitude towards her aunt .

The summer Helen turns sixty, Gena decides to give
her the gift of the sea. She takes a room at the
Waxwoodian Hotel in Waxwood, California with
money she has scrimped and saved from two jobs
and her aunt's disability checks.

But the summer at Waxwood brings to light the
depths of her aunt's mental instability and self-
deceptions about their relationship that she can no
longer ignore.

Before you go...

If you enjoyed this edition of *Gnarled Bones and Other Stories*, please consider leaving a review on Amazon. Even just a line or two would make a big difference and I would be very grateful!

Information on all of my current and upcoming titles can be found at www.tammayauthor.com.